Nobunny's Perfect

Anna Dewdney

PUFFIN BOOKS
An Imprint of Penguin Group (USA) Inc.

PUFFIN BOOKS
Published by the Penguin Group
Penguin Young Readers Group, 345 Hudson Street, New York, New York 10014, U.S.A.
Penguin Group (Canada), 90 Eglinton Avenue East, Suite 700, Toronto, Ontario, Canada M4P 2Y3 (a division of Pearson Penguin Canada Inc.)
Penguin Books Ltd, 80 Strand, London WC2R ORL, England
Penguin Ireland, 25 St Stephen's Green, Dublin 2, Ireland (a division of Penguin Books Ltd)
Penguin Group (Australia), 250 Camberwell Road, Camberwell, Victoria 3124, Australia (a division of Pearson Australia Group Pty Ltd)
Penguin Books India Pvt Ltd, 11 Community Centre, Panchsheel Park, New Delhi - 110 017, India
Penguin Group (NZ), 67 Apollo Drive, Rosedale, North Shore 0632, New Zealand (a division of Pearson New Zealand Ltd)
Penguin Books (South Africa) (Pty) Ltd, 24 Sturdee Avenue, Rosebank, Johannesburg 2196, South Africa

Registered Offices: Penguin Books Ltd, 80 Strand, London WC2R ORL, England

First published in the United States of America by Viking, a division of Penguin Young Readers Group, 2008
Published by Puffin Books, a division of Penguin Young Readers Group, 2010

1 2 3 4 5 6 7 8 9 10

THE LIBRARY OF CONGRESS HAS CATALOGED THE VIKING EDITION AS FOLLOWS:
Dewdney, Anna.
Nobunny's perfect / by Anna Dewdney.
p. cm.
Summary: Bunnies, who slurp their juice, forget to say "please," and bite their friends, learn about good manners.
ISBN: 978-0-670-06288-1 (hc)
[1. Etiquette—Fiction. 2. Rabbits—Fiction. 3. Stories in rhyme.] I. Title.
PZ8.3.D498No 2008 [E]—dc22 2007024008

Puffin Books ISBN 978-0-14-241533-7

Manufactured in China

Set in Shag Mystery • Book design by Jim Hoover

For Reed,

and with gratitude to Beatrix Potter,
who knew bad bunny behavior when she saw it

Every little bunny's good.
They mostly do
the things they should.

But sometimes feeling sad

or mad
can make a little bunny…

Bad bunnies grab.

They do not share.

They hit and kick.
They don't play fair.

They slurp their juice.
They scream and shout.

They burp and spit
their carrots out.

No "please" or "thanks"
or "pardon me."

They fuss and whine
and disagree.

They scratch each other,
squeal, and fight.

Instead of using words
they BITE.

Nobunny's perfect,
that is true–
but aren't you glad
this isn't YOU?

Good bunnies try
to do what's right.

They use their words.
They NEVER bite.

Instead of grabbing,
they say "please."

They're nice to friends
and they don't tease.

They follow rules.
They take their time.
They do not push.
They wait in line.

They say "hello"
and wave "good-bye."

They give a hug
when someone cries.

And when the day
is warm and sunny...
they share it with
another bunny.

No bad bunnies!
No rude rabbits!
Use your manners,
have good habits.
Be polite and kind
and true.

That's my bunny!
Good for you!